KAY THOMPSON'S ELOISE

Eloise Throws a Party!

STORY BY Lisa McClatchy

ILLUSTRATED BY Tammie Lyon

Ready-to-Read

Simon Spotlight
New York   London   Toronto   Sydney   New Delhi

SIMON SPOTLIGHT
An imprint of Simon & Schuster Children's Publishing Division
1230 Avenue of the Americas
New York, NY 10020
First Simon Spotlight hardcover edition September 2018
First Aladdin Paperbacks edition June 2008
Copyright © 2008 by the Estate of Kay Thompson
All rights reserved, including the right of reproduction
in whole or in part in any form.
"Eloise" and related marks are trademarks of the Estate of Kay Thompson.
SIMON SPOTLIGHT, READY-TO-READ, and colophon are
registered trademarks of Simon & Schuster, Inc.
For information about special discounts for bulk purchases, please contact Simon & Schuster
Special Sales at 1-866-506-1949 or business@simonandschuster.com.
The text of this book was set in Century Old Style.
Manufactured in the United States of America 0818 LAK
2 4 6 8 10 9 7 5 3 1
Library of Congress Control Number 2007938994
ISBN 978-1-5344-2038-0 (hc)
ISBN 978-1-4169-6172-7 (pbk)

My name is Eloise.
I am a city child.

I have a dog.

He is a pug.

His name is Weenie.
Today is Weenie's birthday.

I have a big
surprise for Weenie.
I am throwing him a party!

Nanny is helping me
surprise Weenie.

"Oh, Nanny!" I say.
"Weenie and I are
    going for our walk now!"

I give Nanny a big wink.
She gives me the A-OK.

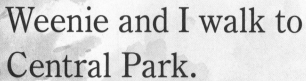

Weenie and I walk to Central Park.

We say hello to all
our horse friends.

Weenie sniffs the flowers.
I pick him a bouquet.

When we get back,
  the manager says,
  "Happy birthday, Weenie!"

He hands me a box.
"For Weenie," he whispers
to me.

I give him the A-OK.

When we get to
our apartment,

Nanny yells,
"Surprise, Weenie!"
I yell,
"Surprise, Weenie!"

Room Service yells,
"Surprise, Weenie!"

The doorman yells,
"Surprise, Weenie!"

The dogs bark,
"Surprise, Weenie!"

"Look, Weenie," I say.

"It's Mr. Afghan Hound
from the twelfth floor!"

"And Spot, the firemen's dalmatian! And Priscilla Poodle!"

"And Doxy,
the manager's
dachshund!"

We all dance around.

Then Weenie and his friends
gobble up doggy biscuits
and bonbons.

Weenie tries to eat the candles on his doggy cake.

He plays
tug-of-war

with his new
doggy toy.

I help Weenie
open his presents.
Weenie plays with
more doggy toys!

Then I give
Weenie my present.

"It is a sweater, Weenie,"
I say.

Then we all curl up
on my bed

and take a good,
long doggy nap.

Oh, I love, love,
love birthdays!